Kylie Jean

Rodeo Queen

by Marci Peschke

illustrated by Tuesday Mourning

PICTURE WINDOW BOOKS
a capstone imprint

Kylie Jean is published by Picture Window Books
A Capstone Imprint
1710 Roe Crest Drive
North Mankato, Minnesota 56003
www.capstonepub.com

Library of Congress Cataloging-in-Publication Data
Peschke, M. (Marci)
  Rodeo queen / by Marci Peschke ; illustrated by Tuesday Mourning.
      p. cm. — (Kylie Jean)
  ISBN 978-1-4048-5961-6 (library binding) — ISBN 978-1-4048-6618-8 (pbk.)
  [1. Contests—Fiction. 2. Rodeos—Fiction. 3. Texas—Fiction.] I. Mourning, Tuesday, ill.
II. Title.
  PZ7.P441245Ro 2011
  [Fic]—dc22   2010030652

Summary: When the rodeo comes to town, Kylie Jean decides she wants to be the Rodeo
Queen! But to do that, she must learn rodeo tricks.

Creative Director: Heather Kindseth
Graphic Designer: Emily Harris
Editor: Beth Brezenoff
Production Specialist: Michelle Biedscheid

Design Element Credit:
Shutterstock/blue67design

Printed in the United States of America in Stevens Point, Wisconsin.
112011
006475R

For Katie Rose, with love for Rick

—M.P.

· Table of Contents ·

All About Me, Kylie Jean!

My name is Kylie Jean Carter. I live in a big, sunny, yellow house on Peachtree Lane in Jacksonville, Texas with Momma, Daddy, and my two brothers, T.J. and Ugly Brother.

T.J. is my older brother, and Ugly Brother is . . . well . . . he's really a dog. Don't you go telling him he is a dog. Okay? I mean it. He thinks he is a real true person.

He is a black-and-white bulldog. His front looks like his back, all smashed in. His face is all droopy like he's sad, but he's not.

His two front teeth stick out, and his tongue hangs down. (Now you know why his name is Ugly Brother.)

Everyone I love to the moon and back lives in Jacksonville. Nanny, Pa, Granny, Pappy, my aunts, my uncles, and my cousins all live here. I'm extra lucky, because I can see all of them any time I want to!

My momma says I'm pretty. She says I have eyes as blue as the summer sky and a smile as sweet as an angel. (Momma says pretty is as pretty does. That means being nice to the old folks, taking care of little animals, and respecting my momma and daddy.)

But I'm pretty on the outside and on the inside. My hair is long, brown, and curly.

I wear it in a ponytail sometimes, but my absolute most favorite is when Momma pulls it back in a princess style on special days.

I just gave you a little hint about my big dream. Ever since I was a bitty baby, I have wanted to be an honest-to-goodness beauty queen. I even know the wave. It's side to side, nice and slow, with a dazzling smile. I practice all the time, because everybody knows beauty queens need to have a perfect wave.

I'm Kylie Jean, and I'm going to be a beauty queen. Just you wait and see!

Chapter One
Spring Round-Up

On Saturday morning, I'm standing on Main Street with Momma, Daddy, and my brothers. The sky is as baby blue as a robin's egg, and there is a cool breeze jiggling the new green leaves on the trees. Bright yellow flowers that look like tiny stars are popping up everywhere. Yup, it's springtime, all right!

Today is the Great Spring Round-Up. Once a year, the cowboys have a parade right down Main Street. It happens two weeks before the Wild West Rodeo.

Ugly Brother really likes to come see the cowdogs. He thinks they are something else. I do too. "Did you know a cowdog can make a big ole cow move any ole place?" I ask Ugly Brother.

He answers, "Ruff ruff!" Two barks means yes, and one bark means no.

I wish the parade would hurry up and start so we could see some of those dogs. When the Round-Up starts we'll hear a lot of noise, but I don't hear anything yet. But as I'm peering down the street, I see Pa walking toward us. He's wearing his Western shirt, jeans, boots, and a big cowboy hat.

"Kylie Jean, just look at you in that pink cowboy hat!" Pa calls. He knows pink is my color. He gives me a big squeezy hug. Then he gives Momma one, too.

"Are you ready to see some real cowboys?" he asks.

"Sure am," I say. Just then we hear people start to whoop and whistle.

Daddy's the tallest of all of us, so he can see the farthest down the crowded street. He shouts, "Here they come!"

Soon, I can hear the horses' hooves as they tap-dance down the brick street. I jump up and down, up and down, but all I can see are the backs of a whole lotta folks.

"Daddy, I can't see!" I whine.

Daddy laughs. He asks, "How about a piggyback ride?" Then he bends down so I can jump on his back and hug his neck real tight.

All the people push up to the street just like waves in the ocean. Everyone wants to see!

I can see the tip-tops of the flags carried by the three riders in the front of the parade. The flag on the right is the red, white, and blue of the U.S. of A. In the middle is the cowboy flag. It's brown, with a yellow cowboy riding a bucking bronco. On the left is our very own Texas Lone Star flag.

You have to be a special celebrity to carry a flag. Plain folks just don't get to do it.

The flags are passing us now, but behind them I can see the chuckwagons. The lead wagon has lots of shiny pots hanging down the sides, and it's neater than a pin.

Up on the buckboard, holding the reins, is Pa's brother, Uncle Bay.

"Uncle Bay!" I shout. "It's me, Kylie Jean, from your family!"

He grins and waves at me. I wave back my beauty queen wave: nice and slow, side to side. Uncle Bay is a world-famous chuckwagon cook. He won the National Cowboy Cook-Off. His barbecue is good, but it was his peach cobbler that done it for him. Momma says it tastes like heaven on a spoon.

Next, I see the cows. I yell, "Get ready, Ugly Brother! Here come those cowdoggies!"

"Ruff-ruff, ruff-ruff!" Ugly Brother barks. He runs round and round, so full of excitement that he gets all tangled up in his own leash. Momma can hardly keep him from running right into the cows passing by us.

"You wish you could be a cow doggie, don't you, Ugly Brother?" I ask when he stops running. He doesn't answer me. He's too busy watching cows.

Some of the cows are black, some are brown, and some have white spots on them. Ugly Brother really likes those black and white cows. They look like him, but bigger.

The cow doggies run from one side of the street to the other, barking and showing those heifers who's boss! Ugly Brother is jealous. I can tell just by looking at him.

The rodeo clowns follow the cows. They wear bright, colorful clothes and have white-painted faces with red noses. Some of the clowns roll right down the street in big brown wooden barrels with their heads poking out.

Those clowns scare Ugly Brother. He covers his face with paws and whines. T.J. rolls his eyes. "You're just a big puppy," he tells Ugly Brother. "Real dogs aren't afraid of nothing."

I narrow my eyes. "Don't you worry, Ugly Brother," I say. "We both know T.J. just wants to be the boss of us."

The riders come at the tail end of the parade. Everyone is cheering. Main Street is loud with whistles and whoops.

Momma nudges me. "Look, there's Nanny!" she says.

Nanny is riding a tall, golden Palomino horse and wearing her Western shirt with yellow roses on it. She's also wearing her special Silver Star rodeo belt buckle, the one she won barrel racing.

I wave both my arms. "Nanny, it's me!" I yell. "Your little angel!"

She smiles and blows me a kiss as she passes by. Then, just like that, the last pony passes by us. The parade is over, and it's time to go home.

Chapter Two
Rodeo Dreams

I can hear the crowd in the stands at the Wild West Rodeo. They're all cheering for me.

I'm sitting in my pony in the middle of the arena, wearing my pink cowboy hat with a tiara on the front of it. The diamonds on the tiara sparkle in the sunlight.

The announcer says, "Here is your new rodeo queen, Ms. Kylie Jean Carter! She is a real rodeo star." He pauses and listens to all the cheering. Then he tells me, "Wave to your fans!"

I flash a smile as sparkly as a tiara. Then I wave nice and slow, side to side, just like a real true beauty queen. The crowd goes wild. I ride in a circle all around the arena so everyone can see me up close.

Then it's time for the closing ceremony, and I'm the one carrying the Lone Star flag! But just as I lift up the flag, rain starts to fall, and I feel something rough on my face. I open my eyes and see a big, wet, pink, doggie tongue coming at me.

Ugly Brother licks me again. That's when I realize the truth. I was only dreaming that I was a rodeo queen!

I push Ugly Brother and his slobbery tongue away. "Quit that," I tell him. "I thought I was a real true rodeo queen at the Wild West Rodeo, but it was just a dream. I should have known it, because I don't even have a pony!"

I flop back onto my pillow. Then an idea hits my brain like a red nose on a rodeo clown. Maybe I can be a rodeo queen!

"I think I can make my dream come true," I tell Ugly Brother. "What do you think?" He runs around the room, jumps up, and barks twice.

I hear Momma's voice call, "Kylie Jean, are you awake?"

"Oh no!" I whisper. I push Ugly Brother off the bed. "If Momma catches you on this bed, we're both gonna be in trouble!" I tell him.

"Ruff," he replies. He puts his paws over his face. I can tell he feels mighty bad about being a rulebreaker.

I give him a quick hug. We have a talk about how everyone makes mistakes sometimes. I know he sure is sorry.

That afternoon after church, we go to Lickskillet Farm. While Nanny's mixing up the lemonade, I sit in the sunny kitchen and ask her lots of rodeo questions.

She doesn't know much about the rodeo queen. "All I know is that the queen is chosen from all of the women who compete in the rodeo," she says.

Rats! I don't have a horse. I can't compete in the rodeo! This is gonna be a lot harder than I thought.

Chapter Three
Get a Rope

The next day I wear my pink cowboy hat to school. I think maybe it'll help me come up with something I can do at the rodeo. But even though I wear it all day long, even in gym class, I can't think of anything. Nothing comes to me.

When I get home from school, Ugly Brother is waiting for me in the driveway. He knows we have a lot to do.

But I'm not sure my dream will come true. The Wild West Rodeo is only two weeks away, and I am fresh out of ideas.

I put down my pink backpack and sit beside him. But just as I sit down, he springs up and runs off. He must be chasing Boots, the neighbor's cat.

I close my eyes to think hard. Then I feel something heavy land on my feet.

Something long and brown is coiled on top of my shoes. "Snake!" I shout, trying to jump up.

Then I realize it's only a rope from the garage. Ugly Brother is standing in front of me, looking really pleased with himself.

"Is this for the rodeo?" I ask.

"Ruff, ruff," he replies.

"What do I do with it?" I ask.

Ugly Brother stares at me. He spins around in a circle. Then he stares at me again.

This is a for-sure puzzle. While I'm thinking about it, T.J. comes out to shoot baskets. He says, "What's up, lil' bit?"

"What can cowboys do with a rope?" I ask.

T.J. laughs. "That's easy!" he tells me. "Rope tricks."

I hug Ugly Brother and ask, "Do you think I should do rope tricks at the rodeo?"

He barks, "Ruff, ruff!"

I give him a big squeezy hug and whisper, "Thank you for helping me!"

I know what he wants. He
wants to wear my cowboy
hat! I put it on his head and
pull the string tight, right
under his chin.

T.J. looks over at us. "Take
that pink hat off that dog right now!" he tells me.

"No way!" I say. "He likes it!" I know Ugly
Brother wants to be a real true person.

"That is a boy dog! Take that hat off of him,"
T.J. demands. He adds, "Ugly Brother, what is
wrong with you? Don't let her treat you like that."

I look at Ugly Brother. "Don't you listen to him,
Ugly Brother," I say. "Besides, Daddy wears pink
shirts, and he looks real nice in them. Boys can
wear pink too."

Then I tell T.J., "We're going to the library, so please tell Momma so she won't worry. We've had enough of your attitude."

The library is just four blocks from our house. When we get there, I tie Ugly Brother to the bike rack. He looks real nice in my hat.

"I'll be out soon," I tell him. "Don't you worry one little bit."

Inside, Ms. Patrick, the librarian, smiles when she sees me. Then she puts a finger over her lips and whispers, "Shhhh!"

I didn't even say anything yet! Although it is true that I am known for being loud, on occasion.

"Do you have a book on cowboy rope tricks?" I whisper loudly.

Ms. Patrick nods. She types something into a computer. Then she walks to a shelf and looks around. She finds a book and brings it to me. It has a big star on the front and is called *Star Rope Tricks*.

I pull my library card out of my pocket and hand it to her. "You sure do have lots of interests," Ms. Patrick says as she scans my card and the book.

"Yes ma'am," I say. "I surely do." Then I skip out into the sunshine.

Outside, Ugly Brother has wiggled my pink cowboy hat off. Now it's lying on the ground. I put it on my head.

"Let's go, Ugly Brother," I say. "I can't wait to read this rope trick book!"

As soon as we reach our house, I sit down on the front porch steps with the brown rope coiled up next to me.

The book says to start with a sixteen-foot-long rope. I go to the garage and get Daddy's tape measure.

Ugly Brother tries to hold the end of the tape measure with his paw, but it keeps slipping out as we're trying to measure the rope.

I get so frustrated that I throw the tape measure on the ground. "Ugh!" I say. "How am I supposed to get a sixteen-foot rope if I can't get the dumb tape measure to stay still?"

Then I hear a voice across the street. "Hey, Kylie Jean!"

It's my friend Cole. He lives in a little brown house just across the street from me.

"Hey, Cole," I call back.

"You look mad," he tells me. He starts walking across the street.

"Yeah, I am," I say when he reaches me. I point to the tape measure. "Ugly Brother's tryin' to help me measure, but I guess his paws just won't do the trick."

Cole looks at his hands. "Maybe I can help," he says.

We measure the rope to exactly sixteen feet. Then Cole cuts it with his pocketknife. He hands it to me and asks, "What are you using this rope for, anyway?"

I show him my book. "Got this at the library today," I explain. "I need to learn a rodeo trick right quick."

Cole shakes his head. "Rope tricks are real hard," he tells me. "You better practice a lot."

I laugh. "Looks like jumping rope," I say. "I bet I can figure it out lickety-split."

I pull the rope and make a lasso. But every time I twirl the rope, it falls flat. The rope gets all tangled up.

"You sure are having trouble," Cole tells me. "Maybe rope tricks are not for you."

"It looks easier in the pictures," I say sadly. "I think I'm just too short to make these rope tricks fly."

"Could be," Cole says. "I think you could do it if you practiced a lot. But the rodeo is in less than two weeks."

That's not enough time to learn those tricks, and we both know it.

I'm not a quitter, but I know when I need to change my plan, and it's that time. "What else do cowboys do?" I ask.

"Ride broncos, ride bulls . . ." Cole begins.

"That's it!" I shout. "I can ride a bull!"

Cole raises an eyebrow. Ugly Brother puts his head down and whines.

Chapter Four

Little Bull Rider

The next day after school, Momma makes me a snack. She cuts cheese with a star-shaped cookie cutter and serves it with crackers.

Yum!

Momma and I always sit down and chat for a few minutes while we eat

our afternoon snack. Today my head is full of questions, so I jump right in and start asking them.

I ask, "Did you ever ride a bull? How does Uncle Bay train those boys to ride those bulls? Can I call Uncle Bay on the phone?

She replies, "No, I never did ride a bull, and yes, you can call Uncle Bay. Ask him about training bull riders."

I dial up Uncle Bay right away.

"Howdy," he yells into the phone. There is a lot of noise in the background. I hear whooping and whistling.

I shout, "Uncle Bay, it's me, Kylie Jean. Can I ask you some questions?

"Why, hello, sugar. I'm out at the bullpen," he tells me. "Have your momma or daddy bring you by later."

"All right," I say.

I decide to get all my homework done before Daddy gets home. Then I just know he'll take me to see Uncle Bay at Rocking Star Ranch.

I'm just getting my math facts finished when I hear Daddy's truck in the driveway. Then the front door slams. "Hello! Anybody home?" Daddy calls.

I shout, "Me! I'm home." Then I run into the living room and give him a big squeezy hug.

"What did you do today, sugar?" Daddy asks.

"I learned that spiders and bugs ain't the same, and also that Momma can use a cookie cutter to cut cheese, not just cookies," I tell him. "And I'm all done with my math facts, so can you drive me over to Uncle Bay's ranch?"

Daddy laughs. "Kylie Jean, I don't know what any one of those things has to do with the other," he says. "Why do you want to go to Uncle Bay's ranch?"

"He told me I could," I explain. "I need to ask him a question. It's important rodeo stuff."

"I don't know, sugar," he says. "It's a school night."

"Please, Daddy?" I ask. "I have all my homework done. And Momma won't care as long as we're back in time for supper."

"All right," Daddy says. "I do need to talk to Pa about something. I could just leave you with Uncle Bay for a while, and then come back and get you."

I am as happy as a cow in hay!

Bump-thump-bumpity-thumpity, Daddy's truck bounces along, making a big brown cloud of dust behind us as we head out to the country where Uncle Bay's ranch is. Soon, I see the big gate with the Rocking Star sign on it. There's a giant metal bull in front.

Uncle Bay has a real bull named Diablo. Diablo is famous. No bull rider has ever been able to ride him for more than one minute.

Daddy stops and lets me out. "Thirty minutes," Daddy tells me. "Call me at Pa's if you need me before then."

I smile. "Got it, Daddy!" Then I zip into the barn.

Uncle Bay is inside, brushing a tall black horse. The horse's bridle has tiny silver stars on it.

"Why, hello!" Uncle Bay says.

"I want to ride a bull!" I tell him.

Uncle Bay laughs. "Not a real one," he says.

"Nope, not at first," I say. "I reckon I better practice a little. How do those bull-riding boys learn to do it?

He points to the corner of the barn. "They ride that," he tells me. There's a fake bull in the corner. It's made of some kind of gray metal, and it's taller than me. It sits in a big pile of soft hay.

I head over to take a look at that fake bull. Right away, I know his name should be Thunder. He's the same color as the sky in a storm.

I think Thunder will work for me if it works for boys to learn how to ride bulls. I'm smarter than most boys anyway.

"Tell me everything about riding this practice bull, Uncle Bay. Then I want to get on him," I say.

Uncle Bay shakes his head. "I suppose you can't hurt yourself," he says. "All right, then. Hang onto the bull with one hand, and use the other one up in the air to keep yourself balanced. And squeeze him real tight with your legs, so you won't fall off."

I nod. "Got it," I say. "Now help me up, please. I'm ready to try old Thunder out."

"Is that his name?" Uncle Bay asks. "He never told me."

"Yes, it is!" I say.

Uncle Bay gives me a boost onto Thunder's back.

I hold on tight and shout, "Ready!"

As soon as Uncle Bay flips the switch, that bull swings me right off of him.

Thump! I land on my back in the pile of hay.

"He's a tricky one!" I say, standing up and brushing myself off. "I better try again."

Uncle Bay frowns. "Why are you so interested in bull riding?" he asks.

"I'm riding a bull for my event in the Wild West Rodeo," I explain.

"Huh," Uncle Bay says. "I never knew you were planning on competing in the rodeo."

"Yes sir!" I tell him. "Can you boost me up onto Thunder again?"

"You know, it takes a lot of practice to win a bull-riding competition," Uncle Bay says.

"Yep, I know," I say. "Come on!"

He boosts me up and turns on the bull again. Thunder jerks right and left.

My pink cowboy hat goes flying. Then I go flying. *Thud!* I land in the straw.

Uncle Bay helps me up. "You're not much of a bull rider," he says. He can tell that makes me sad, and he adds, "If you promise to never get on a bull again, I promise to figure out a better plan for you."

I brush off my behind. I'm going to have a bruise! Those bulls mean business.

I think about what Uncle Bay said. He's a good person, and real smart, too. He's someone you can depend on.

"You've got yourself a deal," I tell him. Then we shake on it, right before we hear Daddy's truck coming up the driveway.

Chapter Five
A Pony Named Star

When I walk outside after school the next day, Momma is parked right next to my bus! She waves me over to the van.

"Pa has a surprise for you," she tells me. "Come on. Hop in."

"What is it?" I ask.

Momma laughs. "If I tell you, it's not a surprise," she says. "Right?"

I shake my head. "But you could just give me a clue," I say. "That's not telling."

Momma doesn't give me a single tiny clue. The whole way out to Pa's, I'm trying to think of what the surprise could be. Maybe they got a new swimming pool in the backyard! Or what if Pa built a playhouse with real lights that work, like my cousin Lucy and I always ask him for?

Momma and I listen to 100.5 on the radio on the way to the farm. That's the station for the most country hits. Country songs tell some mighty good stories, if you listen. I sing some of the words, and Momma does too, but she still won't give me one itty-bitty clue.

When we get to the dirt road that goes to the farm, Momma looks at me in the rear-view mirror. She asks, "Do you have it figured out yet?"

"No ma'am," I tell her.

She parks the van and points. "There's your first clue," she says.

There are three horse trailers parked by Pa's barn.

"Is Pa gettin' a new horse?" I ask.

Momma winks. Suddenly, an idea hits me like red paint on a barn.

I shout, "My surprise is a horse!"

Momma points toward the barn, where Pa is talking to some cowboys. "It's not my surprise to tell," she says. "Go ask Pa what he has for you."

I run to the barn as fast as I can. My pigtails flop on both sides of my head, and my sparkly gold star barrettes almost fall out. When I get close to Pa he holds up his hand.

I am out of air after all that running. Breathing hard, I ask, "What's my surprise? Is it a horse?"

The cowboys wink at Pa and walk into the barn. "You better catch your breath and wait for your momma," Pa tells me.

I hop around like I have fire ants in my pants. "Hurry, Momma!" I yell.

Momma strides quickly over to the barn. She hugs Pa.

"Okay, we're ready," Pa shouts.

The cowboys come out of the barn, leading three of the prettiest ponies you ever did see. The first is a Paint pony with colorful spots on it. The second is white like snow. The third is a gold Palomino pony. She has a white spot on her forehead that's shaped like a star. When the sun hits her mane, it shimmers like a blaze of fire. She reminds me of a comet or a shooting star.

When I see that third horse I nearly burst from excitement. "Do I get to keep one, Pa?" I whisper. "Can it be any one I want?"

Pa puts his hands in his overall pockets. Then he nods. "Yup," he says, grinning.

"Wow!" I say. I step closer to the horses. This is going to be hard!

The Paint pony is cute as can be. She's a white horse with tan, black, and brown marks.

I like the pure white horse a lot, but I'm kind of a messy girl. A white horse would get dirty real quick.

Then I look at that gold horse, the one with the star on her forehead. She snickers and turns toward me.

I gasp. "Momma, did you see that?" I ask. "She knows I'm thinking about her. I bet she wants me to pick her!"

"You better get closer," Momma says. "A horse and a rider have to be best friends. Go right up to her and see how you two get along."

Pa puts two perfect lumps of sugar in one of my hands and a carrot in the other. He says, "You better take that pony a little present."

I walk over slowly, so that I don't spook the pony. First, I put the hand with the sugar up where she can smell it. I feel her velvety wet nose as she sniffs the sugar.

When she nibbles the sugar up, it tickles!

"You can be my pony," I whisper. "We'll be best friends. You'll live here at Pa's house and I'll come and see you all the time. Okay?"

The pony tosses her mane and whinnies. Pa laughs, and it rumbles out over to the barn. Momma laughs, too.

I run over to give Pa a big squeezy hug.

"Thank you so much!" I say. "You've made me the happiest girl in the whole wide world!"

"You're welcome, sweetheart," Pa says. "But you better thank your Uncle Bay, too. He called me last night and told me you needed a horse. I've been thinkin' about gettin' another pony, so I thought this would be the perfect time."

I knew I could count on Uncle Bay. He's the best!

The other ponies are looking a little sad, so I go over and pat their noses.

"Don't worry," I tell them. "You're both real pretty. Some other girl will choose you, and you'll be best friends with her." Then the cowboys lead the other two ponies away.

"Now you need to choose a name for your pony, Kylie Jean," Pa tells me.

I already know her name. I knew it from the first moment I saw her golden mane and the spot on her forehead.

"Star," I say. "Her name is Star."

Star raises her head and looks at me with her big brown eyes.

"See? She likes her name!" I say, smiling.

"There's one more thing," Pa says. "Go on and look in the barn."

I walk over to the barn and head inside. It's dark in there and smells like hay. I see a shape on the floor right next to one of the stalls.

When I look closer, I can see that it's a saddle. It's black, with pretty little pink stars on the sides. Perfect for me and Star!

It smells like leather, and there's a note on it.

The note says,

Kylie Jean,

Pa thought you would need a smaller saddle. You'll always be my Rodeo Queen. Love you bunches,

Daddy
XOXO

It's perfect! I can't wait to give Daddy a big hug.

"All right, we've got to get home," Momma says when I come out of the barn. "Say goodbye to Star."

"Already? But I just met her! She'll be scared here all alone without her best friend!" I say.

Momma says, "Hop in the van, honey."

"Pa, can't I stay in the barn with her tonight?" I ask.

"No, sweetheart," Pa says. "But you can come over tomorrow after school and go for a ride. Don't you worry. I'll take good care of your pony."

"All right," I say. "Bye, Star. Don't feel lonely. I'll be back soon."

I get in the van, and Momma and I talk about how school went and what Momma might make for supper. But all I can think about is my pony.

My pony. Those are the best words in the whole entire world!

Chapter Six
Follow Directions

Before I know it, Star and I are best friends. I ride her every day after school.

She can walk, trot, and gallop. When I pull the reins gently, she follows my directions and turns. She goes where I ask her to go.

I always bring her a treat, and she likes me just as much as I like her.

A few days after Star arrives, Uncle Bay is talking to Nanny when I get done with my afternoon ride through the fields of Lickskillet Farm. They both smile when they see me.

"You're doing a great job ridin', and I think you're ready for part two of my plan," Uncle Bay tells me. "If Nanny trains you to barrel race, you just might win at that rodeo."

"That's a great idea!" I say. "Nanny was the best barrel racer in the whole state of Texas!"

Nanny smiles at me. "It's been a real long time since I was a barrel racer, honey, but I'll try to teach you everything I know," she says. "But you have to pinky swear to work hard at training, follow directions, and never cry or quit."

I make my face serious. Then I reply, "Yes, ma'am. I promise." Then I lean over from Star's back so that we can lock our pinky fingers together.

"We're going to win," Nanny whispers. "Just you wait and see!"

"I bet you will," Uncle Bay says. He smiles at me and kisses Nanny's cheek. Then he touches the tip of his cowboy hat, walks to his truck, and drives away.

"Let's get started!" Nanny says.

"Okay," I say. "What should I do first?"

"Dismount," Nanny says. She grabs Star's reins.

"But aren't I supposed to learn how to barrel race?" I ask. "How can I do that if I'm not on my horse?"

"Your job is to follow directions," Nanny says. "Mine is to teach you. Remember?"

"Yes, ma'am," I say.

We tie Star to the fence. Then, using a stick, Nanny draws three big circles in the dirt, in a triangle shape. "You'll need to pretend these are barrels," she explains.

"Do I ride Star around the circles?" I ask her.

Nanny shakes her head. "Not yet," she says.

I watch as Nanny uses the reins to lead Star around the barrels. First she loops around the left circle, then the right, and finally the one at the top. Star's hooves and Nanny's boots have made a huge clover shape in the dirt.

"Did you see how to lead your horse?" Nanny asks. I nod, and she goes on, "You'll have to walk her around the barrels until she can run them on her own. Come on over here and give it a try."

I take the reins. At first, it's strange to walk Star instead of ride her, but after a while, we start getting used to it.

The next day, there are barrels set up where Nanny had drawn the circles. Pa brings the barrels and sets them up right where Nanny marked the dirt. We keep on practicing, walking around and around those barrels.

It's boring. Star and I don't complain or quit, but sometimes we kind of want to.

By Friday, I'm really bored of walking. There's just a week left till the rodeo. But when I get to Lickskillet Farm after school, Nanny has a big grin on her face. "I think your pony is ready," Nanny says. "You can try to ride her through the barrels now. You've done a great job training her."

"Yay!" I shout. I give Star the lumps of sugar that were sticking to the inside of my jacket pocket. "You're a good girl, Star," I whisper in her ear.

Star whinnies. Then I climb up in the saddle and turn her to face the pasture. Nanny watches from the fence.

That's when I notice that the barrels are missing. "Where are the barrels?" I ask Nanny. "We can't barrel race without any barrels!"

"Star knows where to go," Nanny tells me. "Besides, you need some chaps before you can ride around the barrels. You might get too close and hurt your legs."

Star starts walking without my lead. I call, "Whoa!" and she slows down right away.

I lean down to Star's ear and her mane tickles my face. "You are the best pony in the whole wide world, and we are going to be fantastic! You know what to do, so let's make Nanny proud of us!" I whisper.

Star nods her head. Then she starts walking around the imaginary barrels.

Pa comes out to watch. Star and I are really getting good at making the loops. She begins to run through the loops faster and faster. I lean forward with my hands tangled into the reins as we arc in and out.

The wind is blowing my hair, and the sun is warm on my back.

It feels like we're flying!

When we get to the end of the loops, I lean to the side and give my beauty queen, wave nice and slow and side to side. Then Star tosses her mane. It sparkles in the sun.

Star and I know how to put on a show!

Chapter Seven
Estrella Guesses

That night, I get to sleep over at Granny and Pappy's house. After I get home from the farm, I have a quick snack with Momma. Then I hear a horn. *Toot! Toot!*

"That must be Granny," Momma says. "You better get a move on."

I grab my overnight bag. It's so cute. It's pink and has hearts and stars all over it. Then I run outside and slide into the backseat of Granny's car.

"Hi, Granny!" I say, buckling my seatbelt.

"Hi, sweetheart! You ready to have fun?" Granny asks. She waves to Momma and starts driving away.

"Tonight we'll have a movie night," Granny tells me. "Tomorrow, we'll go to Suzie Q's Diner for breakfast, and then we'll go shopping at Boots Western Wear. We need to get you ready for the rodeo!"

"Can we have pizza for dinner?" I ask.

"Yep," Granny says. "I already made the dough."

"Can I stay up late? And can I call the farm so I can tell my pony good night?" I ask.

Granny laughs. "Yes, you can stay up late. But I don't know about calling your horse."

"What do I need from Boots Western Wear?" I ask.

"You need lots of stuff! I talked to your momma, and since your birthday is coming up, this will be Pappy's and my present for you," Granny says.

"That's right nice of you, ma'am," I say. "You are the best granny in the whole world!"

"What are you going to wear for the rodeo?" Granny asks as she parks the car in her driveway.

"I'm gonna wear my black jeans," I tell her. We walk up the driveway to her house. Her big old house is the same color as the sky. That's where my daddy lived when he was a boy. "And I have a pink cowboy hat already," I add.

"Pink is your color," Granny says.

"That's right!" I say. "Do they make black chaps? I don't want brown ones. They're boring. And my outfit is black and pink."

"We'll just have to see what they have at Boots," Granny tells me. "Go on and put your bag in the pink room."

I run up the stairs. The pink room is where I always sleep when I'm at Granny and Pappy's house. It has pink walls and a really big bed covered with the softest blankets you ever felt. I put my bag on the bed. Then I run back down to the kitchen.

A big blue bowl full of pizza dough is sitting on the counter. Granny spreads flour on the counter and rolls the dough out into a big circle.

Then she spoons bright red tomato sauce onto the dough. "Do you want to do the toppings?" she asks me.

"Yes, ma'am!" I say.

I sprinkle cheese on top of the red sauce.
Then I make a big star out of little circles of spicy
pepperoni. It looks yummy already.

Just then, Pappy walks in. "There's my pretty
girl," he says, giving me a kiss on top of my head.
"Make sure you put a lot of cheese on that pizza.
That's my favorite part!"

"You got it,
Pappy!" I say,
dumping the rest of
the cheese on top of
the pepperoni star.

We eat pizza while we watch our movie. I want
to stay up real late, but by the time the movie
ends, my eyes are starting to feel real heavy, and
I keep accidentally falling asleep.

Pappy carries me up to the pink room and Granny tucks me in. I open my eyes one last time to see the dark, starry sky out the window, but the next thing you know, it's morning!

It's early! The chickens are barely awake, and the rooster hasn't even crowed yet when Granny taps on the pink room's door. "Time to get up, honey pie," she says. "We have a lot to do!"

I get dressed fast. After a breakfast of scrambled eggs, bacon, and biscuits at Suzie Q's Diner, Granny and I are off to Boots Western Wear.

Knowing how to be a barrel racer is just one part of being in the rodeo. I have to look good, too!

"I bet we'll be able to find a pink bandana," Granny says as we walk over to Boots. "Boots has everything a little cowgirl could want."

Inside the store, a salesgirl comes over to us. Her nametag says "Estrella."

"Can I help you two find anything?" she asks.

Granny smiles proudly. "My granddaughter is going to be barrel racing in the rodeo next weekend," she says. "We need a shirt, chaps, and boots."

"I can help you with that," Estrella says. She smiles at me. "How exciting to be in the rodeo!"

Right away, she finds a real cute pink shirt on a rack.

She holds it up to me and says, "I think this is your size."

"I love it!" I tell her. "Now let's look for a pair of boots."

On the way to the boots section, Granny picks up a bandana. It's just the right shade of pink. She twirls it in the air. "I told you they'd have a pink one," she tells me, winking.

All of the boots smell just like my new saddle. I see red boots, blue boots, black boots, and some boots with designs on them. Then I see the perfect pair. They are pink with black stitching and little black stars on the sides. "Let me find your size," Estrella tells me.

I wait on a bench until Estrella comes back with a box. When I slide my feet into the beautiful boots, I feel like Cinderella when she tried on the glass slipper.

"They fit me perfect!" I whisper.

Granny nods. "They're perfect in every way," she says.

I don't want to take them off. Estrella can tell I love them.

"You can put your old shoes in here," she says, handing me the box. "I can tell you'll be wearing your new boots out of the store!"

Granny carries the box, the shirt, bandana, some chaps, and a belt, to the counter.

Estrella smiles at me as she rings everything up. "You're going to look like a real, true rodeo queen!" she says.

I gasp and look at Granny. How did Estrella guess my dream?

Chapter Eight
Barrel-Racing Girl

On Sunday, it's time to practice again. Momma, Daddy, T.J, and Ugly Brother all come to Lickskillet Farm to watch. They stand next to the fence with Pa while I show Star my new boots. She loves them! I can tell because she whinnies really loud when she sees them.

Sitting straight and tall in my saddle, I wait for Nanny's directions. We only have five days left to practice, so we need to get down to business.

"Remember, the fastest rider wins," Nanny tells me.

"Yes, ma'am!" I say. "I aim to be the fastest rider at the rodeo, so don't you worry!"

Pa calls over, "You look the part. I thought you were a regular cowgirl when you got out of the car!"

Daddy has Ugly Brother on a doggie leash. If we let him go, he will chase after me and spook Star. Then I could fall or get hurt.

"Sorry, Ugly Brother," I holler. "Doggies can't ride horses. You just watch me, okay?"

He barks, "Ruff, ruff." That means yes.

Star and I run through the barrels, making careful, small loops. If you make your circles too big, you lose time. The fastest rider wins, I tell myself. The fastest rider wins.

Momma smiles and gives me a thumbs-up. When I finish, she claps. Daddy claps too, and yells, "You're fantastic, baby girl!"

T. J. shakes his head as I ride over to the fence. "I can't believe it," he says. "You're going to win."

My eyes go to Nanny. She's the one who knows what a real rodeo barrel racer needs to do to win.

Nanny's face is stretched into a huge smile. "You get two gold stars for the fastest time yet!" she tells me.

"Let's try it again!" I say.

I keep on practicing until it's time to go home for supper. Every time I'm away from Star, I miss her. In the car on the way home, I ask, "Can we keep Star in our backyard?"

Daddy laughs. "That would be fun, wouldn't it?" he says. "But I don't think our neighbors would like it too much."

"I know you're right," I say sadly. "She might try to eat Miss Clarabelle's flowers or swim in Cole's swimming pool."

"That's right, honey," Momma says.

"I guess she can stay at the farm," I decide.

Chapter Nine
One More Week

On Monday after school, Cole comes to the farm with me. He watches while I ride through the barrels. I do it ten times. Every single time is as perfect as can be!

Cole looks surprised. "You really did it, Kylie Jean!" he says. "You learned how to do a rodeo event." Then he adds, "You're really good at it, too!"

I know he didn't think I could do it. I don't care. I proved him wrong!

* * *

On Tuesday, Uncle Bay comes out to watch me practice. Star and I are ready. We put on a great show.

When Uncle Bay comes over to help me down, he says, "You look just like Nanny did when she was a girl. Don't tell her I said so, but you're even better than she was!" He winks and smiles at me.

"Thanks, Uncle Bay," I say. "I learned everything from Nanny. She's the best! But I won't tell her what you said. It can be our secret."

* * *

On Wednesday, all the farm hands from Lickskillet Farm come to watch me practice. They've been watching me learn to race. Nanny watches with them.

After I'm done, one of them says, "Ma'am, you're a great teacher. Miss Kylie Jean is fast enough to win. I wouldn't be surprised if she sets a record!"

"Nanny is the best teacher in the whole wide world," I tell him. "She gets two gold stars!"

* * *

On Thursday, Granny and Pappy are at the farm when I come over after school. Granny winks at me. "You look like a true cowgirl," Granny says. "But you can't fool me, Kylie Jean. You're doing this just so you can be the rodeo queen!"

I shake my head. "It did start out like that," I tell her. "And I do want to be queen more than anything. But I truly love barrel racing!"

"You're the cutest little cowgirl I've ever seen," Pappy says. "You'll be the rodeo queen. I just know it!"

* * *

On Friday, Nanny and Pa watch me practice. I hardly notice them at all. I'm too busy riding my horse.

Star and I were meant to be friends and ride in the rodeo. She knows just where to go, and I know how to make sure we get there super fast. We make a great team.

But then something happens. I don't know what, but quick as lightning I find myself sitting on the ground, and Star is riding on ahead.

"Whoa, Star!" I shout. "Stop! What happened?"

She stops. I can tell she feels bad that I fell.

Pa runs over and grabs her reins. "I'll take her back to the barn," he tells me. "Looks like she needs a rest."

Tears spring to my eyes. Everything was perfect. Now I don't know if I'll even be able to ride in the rodeo.

"Don't you do that," Nanny tells Pa. "That horse is fine." She rushes over to me. "Are you okay, sugar?" she asks, helping me stand up.

"I think so," I say. "What happened, Nanny? Why did I fall?"

Nanny shakes her head. "I don't know for sure," she says. "I blinked and you were on the ground."

"What if it happens at the rodeo?" I ask quietly.

"It won't," Nanny says. "But if it does, well, that's because people fall while they're barrel racing all the time."

"Not rodeo queens," I say. "Not you."

Nanny laughs. "You think I never fell?" she asks. I shake my head. "Why, Kylie Jean, I've fallen more times than I can count," she tells me.

"What do you do when you fall?" I ask.

Nanny smiles and gives me a hug. "You get back on," she says. "And that's all there is to it."

I nod. "Okay," I say. "I can do it." And I do.

Chapter Ten
Little Cowgirl

The next morning, Ugly Brother wakes me up by licking my face. Finally, it's the day of the big Wild West Rodeo!

My nerves are jumpy as a jackrabbit. It is just getting light out as Daddy and I head to Lickskillet Farm. The sky is streaked with pale blue, gray, and gold. Daddy and I don't say much. It's too early for talking.

When we get to the farm, Pa is sitting on the porch. He's holding Star's brush, a bucket, and some special soap.

I hurry to Star's stall in the barn. She looks just as nervous as I feel.

"Today's our big day," I whisper. "You're gonna want to look pretty."

She whinnies. "I think that means she's ready to get prettied up," Pa says.

First, we wash her. Then I brush her on the low side and Pa brushes her on the high side.

After we're done, Pa stands back. "She really looks like a star today," he says. "Well, your daddy better get you home so you can get a bath and put on your cowgirl clothes."

When we get home, Momma drags me upstairs and dunks me in the bathtub. I scrub the horse smell off of me.

Once I'm dry, Momma braids my hair in one long braid down my back.

I put on my clothes, tie on my bandana, and buckle my belt. Then I slip on the boots with the stars. Next come the spurs and chaps. Finally, I put on my pink cowboy hat. I'm ready!

Daddy has his famous pancakes, bacon, and juice waiting for me in the kitchen.

"You rodeo stars need to eat, too," he tells me, placing the plate in front of me. "I don't want you to be tired when they announce the new queen."

Under the table, Ugly Brother begs for some of my tasty bacon.

"Sorry, Ugly Brother," I tell him, giving him a scratch behind his ears. "I need to eat up today. I need lots of energy!"

Ugly Brother whines softly. Then he walks out of the room.

"Are you excited for today, Kylie Jean?" Daddy asks.

"I sure am," I say. "I really hope I win."

Momma frowns. "Honey, I hope you win, too," she says. "But if you don't, you know you need to be gracious. And if you do, you need to be kind to the other girls, and tell them they did a great job, too. Okay?"

"I will, Momma," I say. "Should I tell their horses, too?"

Momma smiles and replies, "Yes. Horses too. Now eat up. We better get a move on."

"Can I ride in Pa's horse trailer with Star?" I ask.

Daddy laughs. "No, puddin'. You'll ride in the van with me and Momma."

"We'll meet Pa and Star at the rodeo," Momma tells me.

At nine o'clock on the dot, we get to the rodeo. Nanny, Pa, and Star are already there.

The place is packed! Cowboys and cowgirls are everywhere. Everyone is rushing around. I see horses and ponies and cows and bulls in trailers.

The air smells like fresh hay and horses. I hear music playing and people laughing.

I'm so excited!

After I sign in, Nanny gives me a program. "Barrel racing is in the second half of the show," she tells me. "First we'll watch the roping events. After that are the timed events, like goat tying and steer wrestling. Barrel racing is one of the timed events, too."

"After that, is it over?" I ask.

Pa shakes his head. "The last events are the rough-and-tumble ones," he explains. "The most exciting and most dangerous ones, like bronco and bull riding."

"The Grand Entry is first," Momma tells me. "You better get ready!"

Pa leads Star to me, and I mount up. Momma holds up a mirror so I can make sure my hair looks just right. Then I wave to my family. "We're so proud of you!" Daddy says.

Music starts playing. I pull the reins to turn Star around, and we line up with the other riders.

The people watching all cheer and whistle as the Grand Entry begins. I'm near the end of the line, so I have to wait a while before Star and I start moving.

There are three celebrity riders at the beginning of the line. They carry the flags, just like in the parade. One of them is last year's rodeo queen.

I lean down and pat Star's neck. "Next year we'll be the ones carrying the flag," I tell her. "When I'm the rodeo queen!"

When Star and I finally get moving, I feel my heart start to pound. It's kind of scary riding in front of so many people.

I see Momma, Daddy, Pa, Nanny, Granny, Pappy, T.J., Miss Clarabelle, Cole, and all my aunts and uncles and cousins in the stands. I even see Estrella, from Boots Western Wear! She waves when she sees me.

Since I see so many friendly faces in the crowd, I feel better. I don't have to be nervous.

After the Grand Entry, we have to wait for a long time. Finally, a voice booms through the arena. "Riding Star, it's Kylie Jean Carter!" We're next!

Star goes to the center of the arena. "We're going to go around the barrels just like we practiced," I tell her. "Pretend we're in the pasture at Lickskillet Farm. You don't have to be scared. Just pretend it's me and you, nobody else. We can do this!"

We're off! I nudge Star, and we race to the left.

After a quick loop around the barrel, we gallop around the barrel to the right. Then we arc around the barrel at the top. It feels just like riding at the farm.

Before I know it, we're at the finishing line.

I pull the reins gently. "Whoa, Star!" I call. "It's time for our big finish!"

Smiling, I turn to the judges. I give my beauty queen wave, nice and slow, side to side. Star raises her head and tosses her shiny, golden mane.

The crowd goes wild!

I look for Nanny in the stands. When I see her, she's holding up ten fingers. Pa is next to her, holding up two fingers.

That means twelve seconds total racing time. That's a record-breaking time! Yeehaw!

I am so happy. Even if I don't become the rodeo queen, I made my best time ever. This is a great day!

Chapter Eleven
Rodeo Queen

The announcer says, "Folks, we have a brand-new barrel-racing record of twelve seconds flat for Miss Kylie Jean Carter. She's only eight years old! Can y'all believe it? This little gal is something else!"

Everyone cheers and claps and whistles for me. I am so happy!

I brush Star, and then give her some hay. Then I head into the stands.

When I get to my family, Pappy gives me a high-five. Everyone is so proud of me.

Momma, Granny, and Nanny keep on hugging me, and Daddy tells all the people around us that I'm his little girl.

We watch the bronco riding and bull riding. It's exciting, but I can't really pay attention. All I can think about is being the rodeo queen. Finally, the last rider finishes. There are no more events. It's time to find out who the next rodeo queen will be.

"How long does it take them to decide on the queen?" I ask Nanny.

"It's never taken this long before," she replies. Her face looks worried.

I bite my bottom lip. Momma pats me on my back. "Now, you know that they usually pick a grown-up girl for rodeo queen," she tells me. "So don't be disappointed if —"

But the announcer's voice drowns her out. "For the first time ever, folks, we have a little rodeo queen. She stole our hearts when she gave us that wave at the end of her event."

Momma gasps. Granny smiles. Nanny claps. Pa takes his hat off. Pappy whoops. Daddy grabs my hand. Even T.J. looks excited. My heart practically stops!

The announcer continues, "That's right. Miss Kylie Jean Carter is our queen. Come on down here, Kylie Jean!"

Before he finishes talking, I run down to the center of the arena, shouting, "It's me! It's me!"

The Yellow Rose of Texas plays real loud over the loudspeaker. Everyone in the whole arena stands up.

The rodeo queen from last year takes off her sparkly tiara. The front has pretend diamonds and other pretty jewels. She sets it on top of my pink cowgirl hat. Then she whispers in my ear, "You'll be a wonderful queen, Kylie Jean."

I give the folks in the stands my best beauty queen wave. Everyone cheers.

Then Daddy walks out to the center of the arena. He's leading Star and carrying a bunch of yellow roses. "I knew you could do it, baby girl," he tells me. "You're going to be a fantastic rodeo queen."

I give him a big hug. Momma blows me kisses from the stands. Even T.J. is standing up and cheering.

Daddy helps me into my saddle. I lean down, careful not to crush my beautiful roses, and kiss Star on the neck. Then I slip her two lumps of sugar.

"We're both stars now," I whisper. "You're the best pony ever. Thank you for helping me win."

We lead all of the cowboys, cowgirls, and riders around the arena.

I wave and blow kisses to the crowd. The folks go wild, chanting, "Kylie Jean, Kylie Jean!" And Star lifts her head high as she carries me around the arena.

* * *

Later that night, I'm in bed, thinking about the rodeo. Ugly Brother is on the bed, too. (Don't tell Momma, okay?)

"I sure wish you could've seen me ride around those barrels, faster than lightning," I tell Ugly Brother. "Star was a perfect pony."

He barks twice.

"I love my new sparkly crown," I go on, "but I'm still not a real beauty queen yet. Do you think I can do it?"

Ugly Brother barks twice again.

I put my cowboy hat on top of Ugly Brother's head and pull the string tight up under his chin. He looks kinda sad to be wearing my pink hat again. I give him a big kiss. Then he licks me.

"No licking on the mouth!" I shout. "I'm a queen now, so you have to follow my orders!"

Ugly Brother snuggles down next to me in my fluffy pink bed. With the stars twinkling outside, I drift off to sleep, dreaming about being a real, true beauty queen.

Marci Bales Peschke was born in Indiana, grew up in Florida, and now lives in Texas with her husband, two children, and a feisty black-and-white cat named Phoebe. She loves reading and watching movies.

When **Tuesday Mourning** was a little girl, she knew she wanted to be an artist when she grew up. Now, she is an illustrator who lives in South Pasadena, CA. She especially loves illustrating books for kids and teenagers. When she isn't illustrating, Tuesday loves spending time with her husband, who is an actor, and their two sons.

Glossary

bridle (BRYE-duhl)—the straps that fit around a horse's head and mouth and are used to control it

bronco (BRONG-ko)—a type of wild horse

buckboard (BUK-bord)—a horse-drawn carriage

bullpen (BULL-pen)—a secure area where bulls are kept

chaps (CHAPS)—leather leggings that fit over jeans and protect the legs of people riding on horseback

chuckwagon (CHUHK-wag-uhn)—a covered wagon that serves as a portable kitchen

dismount (diss-MOUNT)—to get down from a horse

Paint (PAYNT)—a type of horse with patterns of dark and light hair

Palomino (pal-oh-MEE-noh)—a horse that has a gold coat and a white mane and tail

reins (RAYNZ)—straps that attach to a bridle to control a horse

saddle (SAD-uhl)—a leather seat for a rider on the back of a horse

steer (STEER)—a young male of the cattle family

Talk!

1. In this book, many people help Kylie Jean. Who do you think helps the most? Explain your answer.

2. What was the hardest thing Kylie Jean had to do in this book?

3. What do you think happens after this story ends?

Be Creative!

1. Draw your dream horse. How big is it? What color is it? Does it have any special marks? Write a paragraph describing what you and your horse would do. Don't forget to give your horse a name!

2. Who is your favorite character in this story? Draw a picture of that person. Then write a list of five things you know about them.

3. Kylie Jean's grandmother was a Rodeo Queen. Write about your grandmother. (You might need to ask your parents for help.) What was she like when she was your age?

I made these star-shaped cookies with my mom to celebrate my big day. You can make them too! Don't forget to ask a grown-up for help.

Love, Kylie Jean

From Momma's Kitchen

RODEO QUEEN SPARKLING STARS
Makes: 16 cookies

YOU NEED:

1 grown-up helper

1 16-ounce tube of refrigerated cookie dough (sugar cookie flavor)

1 star-shaped cookie cutter

Sugar sprinkles in your favorite colors

A cookie sheet

A rolling pin

Ask your helper to preheat the oven to 350 degrees.

1. Roll the cookie dough out on a lightly floured surface.

2. Use the cookie cutter to cut out star shapes. Save the extra dough. You can roll it out again to get more stars.

3. Put each star shape on the cookie sheet. Dust with sugar sprinkles.

4. Ask your helper to bake the cookies for 7-11 minutes, or until the cookies are lightly browned around the edges.

Let the cookies cool before eating. Yum-o!

Kylie Jean

has one BIG dream . . .
to be a beauty queen!

Available from Picture Window Books

www.capstonepub.com